P9-AQW-811

To my mom, Marty,
and in memory of my dad, Bernie.
—D.P.

To my husband, David,
and our children, David and Sarah.
—L.B.

STERLING and the distinctive Sterling logo
are registered trademarks of Sterling Publishing Co., Inc.

Library of Congress Cataloging-in-Publication Data

Pilutti, Deb.
  The city kid and the suburb kid / Deb Pilutti ; illustrated by Linda Bleck.
      p. cm.
  Stories are printed back-to-back and inverted.
  Summary: Two cousins, one from the city and one from the suburbs,
  spend a day and a night together at the other's house, and each decides
  he likes his own home better.
  ISBN-13: 978-1-4027-4002-2
  ISBN-10: 1-4027-4002-6
  1. Upside-down books--Specimens. [1. Cousins--Fiction. 2. Suburban life--Fiction.
  3. City and town life--Fiction. 4. Upside-down books.] I. Bleck, Linda, ill. II. Title.

PZ7.P6318Ci 2008
[E]--dc22
                              2007025447

Published by Sterling Publishing Co., Inc.
387 Park Avenue South, New York, New York 10016
Text © 2008 by Deb Pilutti. Illustrations © 2008 by Linda Bleck.
Distributed in Canada by Sterling Publishing C/o Canadian Manda Group,
165 Dufferin Street, Toronto, Ontario, Canada M6K 3H6.
Distributed in the United Kingdom by GMC Distribution Services,
Castle Place, 166 High Street, Lewes, East Sussex, England BN7 1XU.
Distributed in Australia by Capricorn Link (Australia) Pty. Ltd.,
P.O. Box 704, Windsor, NSW 2756, Australia

Printed in China
All rights reserved

The illustrations in this book were created using gouache and at least 10 brushes!
Designed by Lauren Rille

Sterling ISBN-13: 978-1-4027-4002-2
         ISBN-10: 1-4027-4002-6

For information about custom editions, special sales, premium and corporate purchases,
please contact Sterling Special Sales Department at 800-805-5489 or specialsales@sterlingpub.com

NO MORE HONKING HORNS!

No more waiting in the hot subway station for a noisy train!

Jack couldn't wait to visit Adam in the suburbs for a week.

Adam didn't have to share his room with a little brother.

He had a huge yard with a big oak tree outside his window.

Adam had the perfect life.

When Jack arrived, Adam hardly let him put his suitcase down.

"C'mon! There's so much to do!"

First, they rode through the neighborhood.

Next, they fished and looked for frogs.

They took a ride downtown, explored the shops with Adam's mom...

...and got triple-dip ice cream cones afterwards.

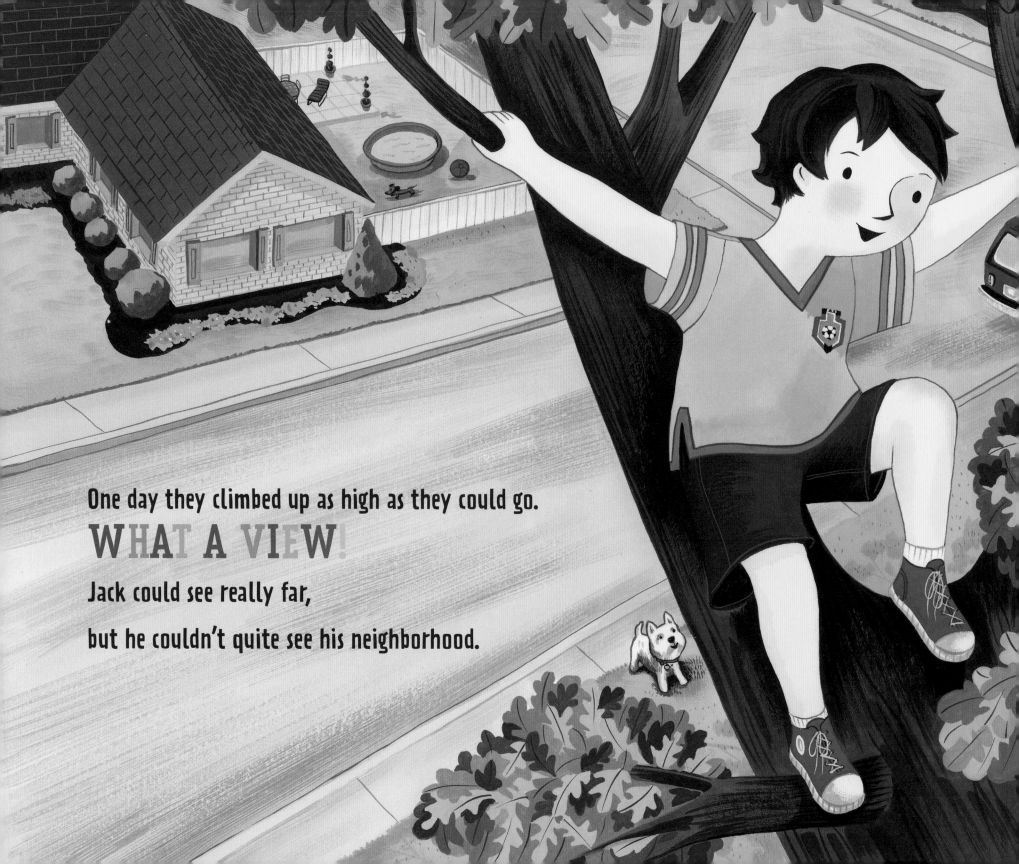

One day they climbed up as high as they could go.

WHAT A VIEW!

Jack could see really far,

but he couldn't quite see his neighborhood.

On the hottest day, Jack and Adam played in the water.

It was fun, but Jack wondered what all his friends were doing.

"Tonight, we'll have the world's best food!"

The food was good, but Jack secretly wished they were having take-out from Mr. Lee's.

They watched a movie and ate a giant tub of popcorn.
Jack imagined that his parents were watching the same
movie at their favorite theater back home.

When he woke up in the morning, Jack remembered something great.

His dad was picking him up today!

Jack couldn't wait to get back to his neighborhood.

He missed his apartment and his room with the perfect view.

He missed the tall buildings. He missed his pets.

He even missed his little brother.

Adam had a nice life in the suburbs, but home was Jack's favorite place.

Now flip the book over to read Adam's story!

Jack had a nice life in the city, but home was Adam's favorite place.

Now flip the book over to read Jack's story!

Adam couldn't wait to get back to his neighborhood.

He missed his house and his room with the perfect view.

He missed the big oak tree. He missed his pets.

He even missed his sister.

When he woke up in the morning, Adam remembered something great.

His dad was picking him up today!

Sleeping outside was scary. Shadows stretched tall and there were all kinds of strange noises.

Jack fell asleep. Adam stayed wide-awake for a long, long time.

the glow of the summer night back home.

It was beautiful, but Adam missed

Adam and Jack stayed up late and watched the lights flicker in the sky.

They watched a movie and ate a giant tub of popcorn.

Adam imagined that his parents were watching the same movie at their favorite theater back home.

"Tonight, we'll have the world's best food!"

The food was good, but Adam secretly wished they were having his dad's famous cheeseburgers.

It was fun, but Adam wondered what all his friends were doing.

On the hottest day,

Adam and Jack played in the water.

One day they climbed up as high as they could go.

WHAT A VIEW!

Adam could see really far,

but he couldn't quite see his neighborhood.

...and got triple-dip ice cream cones afterwards.

They took a ride downtown,

explored the shops with Jack's mom...

Next, they fished and looked for frogs.

First, they rode through the neighborhood.

"C'mon! There's so much to do!"

When Adam arrived, Jack hardly let him put his suitcase down.

Jack didn't have an annoying older sister. He lived in a cool apartment with the tallest buildings in the world outside his window! Jack had the perfect life.

NO MORE LAWNS TO MOW!

No more waiting around for his mom to drive him somewhere!

Adam couldn't wait to leave the suburbs to visit Jack in the city for a week.

Franklin Pierce University

00186661

DATE DUE

GAYLORD

PRINTED IN U.S.A.